Balloon Children

First Edition September 2023
ISBN 979-8-9850823-6-4
ISBN 979-8-9850823-7-1

Published by Nightshade Publishing
NightshadePublishing.com®

Balloon Children

Other Works by Nightshade Publishing®

Through the Violet Redwoods

The Willow Tree Swing

Of Ink & Paper

Stories

And Then What Happened

Kathryn Reilly

Every evening, May's mother would read her stories. When May was old enough, she'd read stories to her mother, buried under quilted blankets her grandmother had made from the most beautiful rainbow fabric scraps. At the end of every story no matter how late it was, without fail, her mother would close the book and ask, 'And then what happened?' And the two of them would imagine lives for the characters beyond the book, sometimes for days.

When she was six, she fell in love with Balto, devouring so many stories of this heroic husky and the other mush dogs. Closing a well-loved library book, her mom turned, smiled, and asked, "And then what happened?"

"Well," May launched in, "Alaska was so thankful for all the dogs' brave service that they built them a doggy castle! It was made of ice of course, because, you know, Husky dogs love cold weather. A huge round room blew snow all day so the dogs could hop in and out of snowy hills indoors until snowflakes became their fur. The canine castle had stairs to walk up but slides to go down. Balto and Fox and Togo would howl sliding down all four slides, one in each corner of the castle. The slides were long and full of turns and the doggies loved them. There was also a room full of bones. Not just regular bones, but giant bones because the people were so thankful they brought bones from all over. Whale bones and elephant bones and bison bones and even a giant walrus bone. Don't worry though, Mom, the animals all died naturally, and then the people brought the bones.

"The dog teams had run so many miles, the people built them a large room filled with soft carpets and covered in old, comfy couches. A fire that never went out kept the room toasty warm and the dogs could lounge, snoring all they wanted, dreaming of the townspeople clapping for them and of the belly rubs they'd have when they woke up."

"Every now and then a squirrel would run through the castle and the dogs would chase it, barking all the time! And chipmunks! And foxes! They loved a good game of chase!"

"I loved that continued story, May. Dream well, I love you. Goodnight." *Click*. Her mom tucked her in and kissed her goodnight.

The next year May's mother indulged her obsession with horses, hosting her daughter's seventh birthday at a farm complete with pony riding lessons. May unwrapped a heavy gift with delight, finding illustrated editions of *Black Beauty*, *Misty of Chincoteague*, *The Black Stallion*, *The Horse and his Boy*, and *The Girl Who Loved Wild Horses* among others. Pages of adventure awaited her, and she was ready.

In a blanket fort with stuffed animals holding court, May closed *Misty of Chincoteague* and sat quietly with her mother for a bit, the flashlight dancing between the blankets enclosing them in imagination enjoying the marshmallowy hot chocolate.

"And what happens next?" Her mom asked, making shadow animals walk along the blanket walls.

"Well," May began, "the horses spoke to each other and decided rebellion was in order. So they sent messages through the seagulls, because the seagulls and horses had long been the best of friends. They asked the snowy-white birds to fly all over the world and question the wisest birds as to how they could grow wings. Because, you see, if the horses had wings they could fly higher than any human lasso, fly far beyond any human's reach. The horses liked their home and they didn't like being driven from it; they liked swimming distances even less. The seagulls agreed and took flight to help their friends.

"They flew through warm, cloudless skies and dark

storm-swirled ones. They rode ocean liners to continents they'd never seen and sought out birds with large wings all over the world, for horses are big and would need the biggest feathers they could find. Mom, what are some of the largest birds in the world?"

"Hmmm. Well I think definitely Marabou Storks and many albatrosses. And we saw Andean Condors at the zoo. Eagles, too."

"Thanks mom. All of those birds, and they also spoke to birds that had never flown. Peacocks and ostriches and kakapos. When describing the horses' request, the birds agreed to help, each donating a single feather. The seagulls returned with feathers of all sizes and shapes and with colors ranging from cerulean blue to bone white. The horses took hairs from their tails and wove all the feathers into a beautiful blanket. As the horses settled into sleep, the seagulls lifted the blanket and covered them, hoping that their friends' dreams would come true.

"All night they dreamed of flying, of cantering through clouds, and playing chase with their feathered friends. They dreamed of wings that wisped through rainbows, of wings that welcomed raindrops and sunshine and wind. And in the morning, when they woke, they had wings; beautiful, long-feathered wings that shimmered in the sunlight holding all the colors of the world."

"What a lovely addition to the story, darling," her mother

softly shared, smoothing out a tangle before her daughter laid her head down and slept. May heard a faint *click*, and she briefly wondered what it was before sleep found her.

The following year May became obsessed with insects, specifically moths after finishing a fantasy series where fairies all had beautiful moth wings: everything from the pale green luna moth wings to the dalmatian-patterned leopard moth's wings. She convinced her mom to set up a moth observation in the backyard, so off to the local hardware store they went to purchase special lights and a collapsible frame to hold a sheet.

Ensuring all the house lights were out, they set up the sheet, turned on the special lights, angling them just perfectly so the light would softly glow through the sheet. Attracted by the brightness, slowly the moths settled upon the sheet, and May documented each with a camera. Settling down in the old swing together, warmed by blankets her mother tucked around them, they watched the small creatures flutter about eating warmed cookies amongst the fireflies and stars.

"If we hadn't stayed up, we'd have never known just how much life lives in the dark," May commented.

"How many different species have you found?" her mother asked.

"At least twenty-seven," May replied, "it's so cool. See this large moth here? The brown-winged one with the beautiful orange and gold coloring? It's a cecropia moth, part of the giant silk moth family; one of the characters in the series I'm reading has its wings."

"Do you like the series?"

"Yeah, I love it. I read it on the bus every day."

"What do you think happens after the story?"

"*Hmmmmmm*. I think the magic goes haywire and the tiny fairies with moth wings grow Godzilla-sized, their wings spanning entire city blocks. They leave the only forest homes they've ever known, determined to save the world. Now that they're large enough, they can do so much more than when their hands were the size of acorns.

"So with their giant wings that can change the course of the winds and dissipate the fog, they set about remaking the world. In synchronicity, they beat the smog back from the cities, making the air crisp once more, carrying the scent of flowers. Using their wings they create tumbleweeds of trash and shepherd them into space until they burn in the heat of the sun. They gave us back our world, walking among us as giants. They control the winds, protecting people from sandstorms and hurricanes and tornadoes; they became the giant protectors of Earth."

Click.

In fifth grade, May began researching Amelia Earhart for an assigned presentation. Back to the library they went, and she checked out a variety of books about the fearless adventuress. After several days of reading and note-taking, she'd created a well-documented presentation. At dinner, May seemed more quiet than usual. "What are you thinking about honey?"

"Amelia's story. You know they never found her plane. What happened?"

"Well, how do you think her story ended?"

"I don't think it ended. I think she and her plane flew into a time warp. One minute she's on course and the next minute she's spiraling through a vortex surrounded by sparkling stars. She emerges in the twenty-sixth century. Amelia doesn't realize this until she lands of course, because the continents are in the same place. Exiting the plane she notices the lack of towering steel and stone structures. Walking into the nearest city she sees green everywhere, and people walking through the air. She witnesses a world reconstructed; bioluminescent creatures light the way; people have saved the planet and equity and equality rain down everywhere. The future welcomes her, but tells her she could never go back to her time; that's why history never found her plane. They embrace her and she lives among them; she gives rides in her now antique plane, flying over a future Earth lush with forests spanning coast to coast. Instead of electricity lighting the night sky, the soft glow of jellyfish floating in giant glass street lamps lights the way. Amelia couldn't believe how dark the world became at night; but she realizes just how bright the stars become and she begins thinking about flying to the stars—without a ship.

"But what she loved most of all, mom, was that future people could fly themselves. They could attach gravity disruptors to the soles of their shoes and fly, up, up to touch the clouds, somersaulting through the cumulus rabbits and brontosauruses and rhinos. So Amelia kept her plane, but she began designing suits to allow adventurers to fly exploring without ships."

Click.

"Wow, May, that sounds like quite the adventure. Would you fly if you could?"

"Nope. I think I'd much rather be telepathic; then maybe I could talk to animals or ghosts or just know what others were thinking."

Smiling, her mom cleared the table. "That's a pretty good what happened next, I have to say. I'd love to be able to fly myself."

Middle school came and went; May kept reading, mostly on her own. But in her head, always in her head, she'd hear her mom's voice ask *And then what happened next?* And her mind would always answer, daydreaming or nightdreaming the characters' lives that came alive to her.

High school ended and suddenly the world unfurled before her. To celebrate, her mom cooked her favorite dinner and having finished, set two wrapped presents before May.

"Go ahead, open them," she smiled.

Tearing off the wrapping paper, May found beautifully bound books set in real and fantastical worlds; she couldn't wait to begin. The second gift, smaller, offered an ornately-carved wooden box. May's fingertips traced over the designs before opening to the lid. Nestled carefully within, she saw dozens and dozens of tapes.

"They're your stories," her mom shared, "nearly every single one since you began sharing them with me when you were three. Remember the one about the duck that learned to drive? And every day he drove the kids to school and taught them how to quack? That's the very first one. Keep them for yourself or turn them into stories and share them with the world. You'll do amazing things May, and I can't wait to hear the stories you'll come up with. Always remember: you're never too old for stories. I wonder what will happen next?"

May smiled, knowing that not knowing was the best adventure of all.

Dream

Alison Clarke

The

         Unicorns

            Are

               Speaking

The

    Unicorns are melting into Fuchsia and grey Silver…

Moon   Light

The Angels   a   r   e

praying

                Smoke   shade

Dreams

The   Unicorns   are

Floating

            In

                                                  The

                                                  Air

        Mountains of words are in the Distance

Shifting and Changing   Shifting and Changing

                                    Morphing

                         Morphing

        The dreams are Alight

                         The

Dreams

      Are   A   B r e a t h

                                        The

Dreams…

            They   Are

A   Treasure

                          The dreams are

Holy   Enshrined

                   As a child,

I   Dreamed

                As an adult,

I   Dreamed

                  They   said   it   Didn't

Matter

                          They

Were   USELESS

                  Insipid

They   Were –

But…   they

                    are

Liquid

Solid

                    They are   Currency

        A   Spark

To   A   Path

        Always   Of

VALUE

        We   Saunter

                                We   Falter

                B   u   t

Always

                                        We DREAM

        always   we

Swim,

                                                Dance,

Alive…

        Yes,   A

Gateway

                                To   Dream

        To   D R E A M

        T   O

        D   R   E   A   M

Moonlit Play

Xanna Renae

Trees swayed with the song in the wind. The setting sun chased by the cool of night. Purples and pinks joined blue in the dance of the sky. And the moon rose steadily over the horizon to taste the last breath of its warm companion.

Frogs and crickets struck up a new tune, accompanying the wind. The fireflies would light the scene. And if one looked carefully, a fairy or two could be spotted playing near tables of mushrooms and rings of rocks.

The potted flowers trickled golden dust as accessories for all who wandered near. The fox lay still and silent for any creature who wandered far. And the moon watched over all, keeping a tally of nature's play.

When the moon grew tired, and the musicians lost their beat, everyone would lay down a while as the moon sunk low. Waiting for the warmth of sun to bring a new game to play.

And the cycle would repeat

and repeat

and repeat.

First Print found in *Through the Violet Redwoods* by Xanna Renae

The Dragon of Twilight Glade

B.R.R Cannon

Elora nudged her bedroom door open and peered into the darkness. She couldn't see it, but her skin crawled as she felt the warm breath of the Black Shadow in her room. Carefully, she reached for the lamp on her dresser. Weeks ago, she had begged her mother to move the lamp as close to the door as possible, and her mother had finally given in to her desperate requests.

With a *click*, the darkness and the Shadow hiding in it vanished. She sighed in relief. Yet again, she had evaded its ominous presence. Her parents had told her that there was nothing there, but she knew better. A monster lurked in her closet, and only light could banish it from her room.

Elora slid under the covers and waited for her least favorite part of the night.

Her mother arrived first. "See? Everything is fine. No monsters."

Elora wanted to tell her that it had been there, but her mother would never believe her. Instead, she nodded.

"Good night, Ellie," her dad said as he joined her mother at the side of the bed. "Sweet dreams."

After the kisses and good nights, her parents returned to the door and gave a final glance back.

"Sleep well, Ellie," her mother said. Then she turned off the light and partially closed the door.

Elora held her breath and worked quickly. While her room wasn't entirely dark, the partially opened closet was. If she was going to fend off the Shadow, she only had a second to do so. She reached under her pillow and shined the flashlight through the black crack. If the Shadow was there, it shrank away, like it always did.

With a sigh of relief, she set the flashlight on the nightstand and pointed it toward the closet. Then, she settled in and closed her eyes. The Shadow wouldn't get her tonight.

◌

Darkness. Elora's entire room was black.

She shot upright and fumbled around for her flashlight. It was still on the nightstand, just where she had left it. She slid the switch up and down, but nothing happened.

Should she run to the lamp? No. There was no more

light coming from the hallway, and that meant the power was out. Nothing would happen. She was about to call for her parents when she heard something in the closet. It was too late. The Shadow was here. She pulled the blankets over her head and held her breath. Maybe if she was quiet, it wouldn't know she was there.

"Ellie?"

The tiny whisper surprised her. She had never heard that voice before, but it sounded… friendly?

"Ellie?"

She pulled down the blanket and squinted, trying to find the speaker, but it was too dark.

A tiny light appeared. A little hedgehog stood there on its back legs, holding a tiny lantern with a front paw. A fairy stood beside it. Elora rubbed her eyes. This couldn't be real.

"I told you we would arrive before the Dragon came back, Reginald," the fairy said.

The hedgehog scoffed at her. "You didn't know that for sure, Clover."

"We don't have time for this. He could come at any moment. Ellie, you must come with us. You are in grave danger."

Elora's mind flooded with questions, but they all vanished when she felt that familiar, ominous presence.

"Hurry!" Clover called.

Before Elora realized what she was doing, she had leapt

to her feet and joined the hedgehog and fairy.

"This way!" Reginald called.

She followed them into her closet and watched as their light vanished behind a small set of drawers in the corner. She peeked behind it and found a hole—just large enough for her to squeeze through—illuminated by the amber glow. She never remembered seeing that hole before.

She knew the Shadow was coming, so she dropped to her knees and followed the tiny light into the hole. Instead of finding herself in the hallway linen closet next to her room, it twisted on for a long way. When she hesitated or tried to pull the hem of her nightgown from under her knees, Reginald and Clover urged her to stay close to the light, so she did.

Finally, the strange tunnel ended, and Elora felt like she had walked into a dream. She was surrounded by the most magical nighttime forest. Tall trees with silvery leaves stretched high above her head, and fireflies danced between them like twinkling Christmas lights. She quickly realized that, among the fireflies, there were more fairies. Their wings emitted a silvery glow as they darted from the treetops and flitted around Elora.

"She is the one! She is the one!" They sang in their tiny voices.

"We can't be late," Reginald called.

With that, all the fairies gently led Elora deeper into the

forest. Soon, she arrived in a starlit glade, surrounded by all sorts of animals: deer, squirrels, birds, and even a few small bears. At the center stood a wizened rabbit.

"Reginald, Clover, you have done well," the rabbit said. "You have brought her safely to us."

All of the creatures voiced their approval.

"It was close," Clover said. "The Dragon was about to arrive."

"Still," the rabbit replied, "you have done well." Then he turned his attention to Elora. "You have explained everything to her then?"

"We had to leave quickly…" Clover began. "There wasn't much time…"

Reginald shook his head and gave a blunt, "No."

Elora glanced around at all of the creatures staring at her. They all had such hope in their eyes. Elora had read enough fairytales to know this meant they expected something of her. Probably something great. Probably something she didn't want to do.

"Ellie," the rabbit continued, "I'm sorry that the situation was not explained to you. I doubt that you were even given my name. I am Hew, and I lead the creatures of the Twilight Glade. As it turns out, we share a common enemy. One that means to destroy all of us."

"The Shadow?" Elora whispered.

"The Dragon, yes," Hew corrected. "There is an old

prophecy that a girl—you—would come and defeat the Dragon with a magical weapon. A sword."

Elora frowned. "Me?"

"Yes, my dear. Your safe arrival is a good omen. Now, we must prepare you to face the Dragon."

Before Elora could voice her confusion or remind them that she was only eight, a group of squirrels dashed down a nearby tree and straight to Hew.

"Hew! Hew! It's coming! It's coming!"

"Hide, everyone!" Hew called.

The rabbit motioned for Elora to follow him into a nearby shrub. She sat as low as she could and held her breath as heavy footfalls approached. Between the thick leaves, she caught a glimpse of dark scales and enormous wings. That familiar, terrible dread followed it. The Shadow. The Dragon. Her heart felt like it would burst from her chest. It *was* real.

Even long after it left, no one in the glade moved. Finally, a dove's coo broke the silence and creatures began to emerge again. Elora reluctantly followed Hew out of the bush.

"What will it do if it finds you?" Elora whispered.

Hew frowned up at her. "I dare not say. But if you have the sword, it can't touch you. Hurry. We must show you what to do before it returns."

✲

"This is it." Hew motioned at the thick hedge.

Elora eyed it. The shrubs were thick—so thick she couldn't see through them—and far taller than her. She doubted that even her father could have looked over it if he was here.

"How do we get in?" she asked.

"Leave it to me," Clover replied as she flitted above their heads. She flew above the hedge and out of sight.

Nothing happened for a while. Then finally, a door made of branches and thick leaves opened before them, revealing a small clearing. In the middle, a sword stood out of a small stone.

Hew, Reginald, and Clover didn't move. Elora took it to mean that she ought to go first. She drew a deep breath and took a few steps forward. The others followed, and Clover closed the door behind them. Elora glanced back at the closed door, wishing that she could go back to her bed, but hat wasn't an option. Not while the Dragon could slip into her room so easily and unleash the terror that Hew was afraid to say.

When she reached the sword, she glanced down at the others. "What am I supposed to do?"

"Have you never read any fairy tales?" Clover asked.

Of course she had. "I have to pull it out?"

"Yes," Hew replied. "Many other creatures have tried over the years, but none of us are large or dexterous enough.

We need a human. *You.*"

Elora sized up the sword. "It would be much easier for someone bigger. I have a cousin who's twelve."

"But the Dragon is not interested in that one," Hew replied. "It must be you."

She nodded uncomfortably. Her cousin's size and love of baseball over books would make him better suited than her.

However, she read enough books to know what she needed to do next. Like King Arthur, she put both hands on the hilt of the sword and gently pulled on it. There was no resistance as it slid up and out of the slit in the rock. Hew, Reginald, and Clover gasped audibly.

"She *is* the one," Reginald whispered.

Elora held the sword up awkwardly. It was heavier than she expected. In books, everyone wielded swords so effortlessly. It would still be a struggle if she was eighteen instead of eight.

As the tip sank back to the ground, Elora looked back at Hew, Reginald, and Clover. "I don't think I can do this. The sword is too big."

The three forest creatures glanced at each other uncomfortably.

"Is it not the right time?" Clover asked.

Hew shook his head. "It is." Then he looked up at Elora. "You can do it. It is said the sword has an engraving on it with words of wisdom for its bearer."

Elora turned the sword and leaned down so she could look at the blade. Sure enough, there were words written down the middle. "'Draw strength from courage and courage will grow. Fear will dwindle until it is no more.'"

She glanced at the others. "What does that mean?"

Reginald and Clover turned to Hew, but the rabbit, Hew, frowned. "I don't know, but we will find out together. Do you have courage?"

She shrugged. She didn't feel courageous. The Dragon was twice her height and as long as her parents' minivan. One swipe of its claws would likely be enough to finish her off. It made the fearsome Rottweiler next door look like a mouse.

Yet the others' expressions held such desperation. They didn't have any hope of fending the Dragon off themselves. None of them were large enough to pick up the sword, not even the bears she had seen in the glade. She had spent so many hours playing the heroic princess. Now, she had to take on the role for real.

"Yes," she finally managed to utter.

The others beamed.

"Good," Hew said. "Now, you must rest before the Dragon returns."

○

"Make yourself at home!" Reginald made a grand bow and motioned proudly to the small cave behind him.

When Hew had told Reginald and Clover to find Elora

a place to rest, this wasn't what she was expecting. She had hoped for a warm cottage outfitted with proper beds or an enchanted castle with friendly furniture and crockery. The pile of green leaves in the corner of a cave didn't fit her idea of comfortable. Especially as she noticed a small cricket emerge from the heap.

"Indeed," Clover scoffed. "This is hardly a place for a child to sleep."

"Then what do you have in mind?" Reginald shot back. "Your little nest in a flower? She won't fit there."

Elora sighed. "This will do just fine. But can we get rid of the bugs?"

Reginald brushed the fur on his face anxiously. "Oh dear. My dinner has escaped again. Sorry about that. Yes, I will take care of them."

In the other corner, she noticed a familiar, colorful tube. "Is that my kaleidoscope?"

He began brushing his face even more vigorously. "Perhaps… You have some interesting things in your closet…"

Elora wasn't sure whether to be upset about or afraid of the constant intruders in her room. "How long have you been sneaking in there?"

"A while. Hew sent us to keep watch over you. You can have it back."

"It's fine. You can keep it. My aunt got me another one last Christmas since this one disappeared."

Clover sighed. "Reginald."

"Yes, yes. I'll tend the crickets now." Reginald vanished into the cave.

"In the meantime, child," Clover said, "we can take a short walk. Don't be long, Reginald."

As Reginald hurried into his cave, Elora followed Clover down a narrow path. Elora shifted the weight of the sword on her back. At Hew's insistence, she carried in a makeshift sheath made out of an oversize leaf and some vines. Finally, they came to the edge of a cliff that overlooked a larger forest. Beyond it, the sun rose, illuminating the fine mist that rested over the canopy. She wondered if the Dragon was hidden down there somewhere or if it was lurking somewhere nearby.

Clover seemed to read her thoughts. "We don't have to fear the Dragon during the day. It only comes out at night. But you already knew that."

Elora nodded. "I told Hew that I had courage, but I'm afraid."

Clover landed on Elora's shoulder and stroked Elora's hair gently. "We all are, my dear. Courage doesn't mean that you're not afraid. It's a choice you make when you are afraid."

Elora's parents had told her something similar before when they tried to console her after a close call with the Dragon. However, every time she imagined standing face to face with it, all she felt was a fear that turned her fingertips cold.

"We may not be able to use the sword to fight," Clover continued, "but we will be there with you. You won't fight alone."

○

Dark nightmares swirled through Elora's mind all day. Her fitful sleep was filled with the Dragon, the sword, and her defeat. Then the claws digging into her arm were replaced with a gentle touch and the snarls with a tiny voice.

"Ellie?"

She shook herself awake. Clover and Reginald stared at her with concern.

"I'm fine," she said. She began to sit up but quickly remembered that the cave roof was far too low for that. Instead, she crawled out of the cave and stood.

"Don't forget the sword." Reginald tried to lift it, but he barely moved the edge of the hilt.

Elora hoisted its bulk onto her back and secured it with the vines again.

Though the trees still glimmered with ethereal light, it wasn't enough to keep the Dragon away. Darkness was falling.

With cold fingertips and a knotted stomach, Elora smoothed out her dirt-covered nightgown. "Which way?"

Reginald and Clover didn't speak as they led Elora back to the glade where she had met all of the creatures before. Everyone had gathered there again. They watched solemnly as Reginald and Clover brought her to the center where Hew sat.

"Are you ready?" he asked.

Elora debated what to say. Finally, she shrugged. "As ready as I'm going to be."

The answer seemed enough for Hew. He seemed ready to share some words of wisdom when a duo of birds dove to his side.

"The Dragon is coming! The Dragon is coming!"

Elora wanted to run and hide, but she forced herself to stay still. To her surprise, none of the other creatures moved either.

"We all stand together today," Hew announced. "As the sword says, 'Draw strength from courage and courage will grow. Fear will dwindle until it is no more.'"

The creatures loudly voiced their agreement.

Then everything fell silent as heavy footfalls began their approach again. Elora watched the others. Still they didn't flee. Instead, they formed a semicircle behind her and stood firm.

Hew still stood at her side. "You can do this."

She removed the sword from her back and unwrapped the leaf from the blade. Then she held the sword up with both hands and tried not to show how much she strained under its weight.

The familiar, warm breath entered the glade, and the Dragon's shadow followed it. Elora felt completely cold, but she forced her feet into a wider position and stared down the Dragon like she stared down the neighbor's Rottweiler when it growled at her on the other side of the fence. She just hoped that, like the Rottweiler, the Dragon wouldn't see through her façade.

The Dragon halted at the entrance of the glade and laughed. She had never heard its voice before, but it was as sharp as its long teeth and dark as its scales. "You choose to stand against me?"

Elora couldn't force her tight throat to make any sounds. She simply struggled to breathe.

"Give me the sword, little Elora," it continued. "Give it to me and I will spare you tonight."

"She will do no such thing!" Reginald shouted. Elora hadn't realized that he stood just behind her right leg.

"Brave little creature," the Dragon replied. "Are you sure? Do you intend to take up the sword yourself if she does?"

Clover whispered a reprimand at Reginald, and he fell silent.

"As I thought," the Dragon said. "Little Elora, put the sword down now."

Elora felt her grip loosen, and the tip of the sword began to sink. It was too heavy to hold for long. There was no way that she could fight with it. Perhaps she should just hand it over and be done with it.

She glanced back at the creatures around her. They remained resolute and even closed in closer around her. They obviously looked to her for help, but they were willing to provide whatever help they could as well. As much as she wanted to run, she had to do something. That's what the heroic princesses in the fairy tales would do. And if they were willing to continue standing by her side, then she would stand by their side too.

She gripped the sword tighter, held the point up toward the Dragon's snout, and took a step forward. "No." The word was little more than a squeak, but she had managed to say it.

The Dragon stepped closer as well. "No?"

Elora cowered at its voice. Then she thought about the fear she had endured: always turning on lights, hiding under the blankets, being told that what she feared wasn't real. Anger and indignation began to boil hot in her chest. No. One way or another, it would end tonight.

"No." Her voice came out a little stronger this time.

The Dragon took another step closer. "You dare to defy me? I could crush you with just one claw."

Did its threat have a hint of uncertainty?

"No," she repeated, louder and bolder.

The creatures behind her moved closer and stood up taller.

"No!" She shouted this time. The cold sensation in her fingers thawed, and the sword didn't feel so heavy anymore.

The Dragon shrank back. Or did it actually shrink a little? It didn't seem twice her height and as long as a minivan. Instead, it looked her eye to eye. It bared its teeth, but even as it did, it looked even smaller. It hardly rivaled the Rottweiler next door.

"I'm not afraid of you!" she yelled, raising the sword. "Not anymore!"

Now the Dragon seemed no larger than a cat. It growled before turning around and running.

The glade erupted into shouts, and half of the creatures chased the Dragon into the forest. As it ran, it seemed to vanish into the leaves on the forest floor.

The rest of the creatures gathered around her. The fairies broke out into song and swirled around her as the remaining animals congratulated and thanked her.

Soon, the rest of the creatures returned. "The Dragon is gone! It has been defeated!"

The celebration began anew until Hew called for their attention. "We must prepare the feast! Everyone, bring what you have and meet back here when the moon is at its zenith!"

With that, everyone else disappeared into the nighttime forest, leaving Elora and Hew alone.

"Is it really over?" Elora asked. The words were little more than a whisper, as though the Dragon might hear them and reappear. "Is the Dragon really gone?"

Hew smiled. "Yes, my dear. I understand the words on the sword now. The Dragon fed on fear, but with no one to fear it, it is no more."

She frowned. "So you didn't really need me in the end, did you?"

"On the contrary! Your fear is what fed it, and your courage is what defeated it. None of us need to worry about it anymore. Especially you. This is your victory, and you are the one we will celebrate tonight."

As dawn approached, so did the end of the celebration. The first glow of light revealed empty tables covered in flowers, berry stains, and nut crumbs. Elora yawned as she adjusted the flower crown woven by the fairies. Then she leaned back against the tree that acted as a backrest. It had been everything she imagined a magical party would be.

"Ellie?"

Elora rubbed her eyes. She must have dozed off at the table. She opened her eyes and sat up, only to realize that she was no longer in the forest. She was back in her room, in her own bed, and light poured in through her window.

Her mother stood in the doorway. "You slept in, Ellie. I think we all did. The power went out last night. Did you sleep okay?"

Elora nodded as she struggled to figure out how she had gotten back home.

"Were you okay even though it was dark?"

Something drooped into her line of vision. She felt the top of her head. The flower crown was still there. She smiled. "Yeah. I don't think I'm afraid of the dark anymore."

"I'm so glad!" Her mother paused. "Where did you get the flower crown?"

Elora laughed to herself. "It's a long story."

Her mother smiled. "I'm looking forward to hearing about it over breakfast."

Fairytales are Dead

Natasha Alva

I used to love playing princess because I thought that it was cute.

Every night, my bedtime stories were about a damsel in distress waiting for her knight in shining armor to rescue her, having special powers that would create good in this world, and ending happily ever after.

It was hard to leave the house without wearing a princess dress and I was doubtful to eat an apple as it might have poison on it.

I used to believe in sprinkling pixie dust so that I could fly.

There were no nuances to believing in these stories because of the thought that dreams will come true.

I was a hopeless romantic wherein having the belief that a true love's kiss exists.

There were even moments of doubt whether going to a forest was a good idea because one might encounter an old hag, an interesting creature, or some other alien.

Call it delusion but sometimes these fantasies did warp my mind.

In every fairytale, there is always a darker truth behind it.

A once upon a time becomes cliché and a happy ever after becomes a myth.

Dreams may become a reality, but they are living miracles.

No wonder Peter Pan never wanted to grow up.

Reality is filled with painful histories with lesser chances of having good endings.

Fairytales give moments of euphoria, but it is only for temporary wage.

Fairytales are dead and I am just living in this bubble until it fades away.

The Underworld

Dani Fankhauser

I didn't tell Mom I hated school because she would never understand. Every weekday she drops us off in the white minivan at 8:22 a.m. and makes a U-ie to go back home. Then she eats cinnamon rolls on the couch, or whatever she does all day, while I'm stuck here in the third row, holding my pee, because my best friend Evie made me play handball all through recess and I don't like the way everyone turns to look at me when I ask for the hall pass.

The bell rang. I shoved my three-ring binder into my navy Jansport backpack, smashing the blue foam lunch box shaped like a paper bag with the textbooks, and zipping the pencils safely into the outside pocket. In the top, I slid my library book, *Bunnicula*, for easy access. The vampire rabbit had a secret life at night but the stupid family dog was out to get him. I wished my family's pet bunny had special powers, but she's just a regular rabbit who tries to dig a tunnel out of her cage sometimes.

The kids shuffled out of the room. I followed, slinging my backpack over one shoulder. Only nerds put both arms through. I did my fast-walk to meet Becca at the big tree. She always got there first. Her teacher lets them out early because they are already fifth graders, and her classroom is closer to the big tree.

It always goes the same. She will be reading a book, we start walking, and I pull her elbow so she doesn't wander into the *No Parking Zone* sign and again at the *Stop* sign on our way down the hill. Then we'll turn right through the crosswalk, through the cul-de-sac, and into the park where Mom will pick us up. I'm sick of Becca and her book. I'm worried someone from my class could see me with her and know that she reads while she walks and think I do that too.

When I was in kindergarten and had half-days, Mom picked me up first. And before I started kindergarten, we'd drop Becca off in the morning and take donuts to the park. I was so excited to start school and get dropped off with Becca because I thought being grown up was better, but it's not.

I crossed the grass by the parking lot on my usual path, careful not to trip on the tree roots, dodging the running kindergarteners who were about to get yelled at. The dirt under my feet felt soft and I froze in place, lightheaded, as if the ground was swaying like a boat. There was a seam in the grass next to my left shoe. I follow the line around in a slow circle. It was the size of a tire swing.

People could look at me weird. I knelt down on the grass. All instinct. I dragged my finger along the line. Still, my heart was pounding, because I'd look really dumb if I'm wrong.

All the chatter and laughter, the cars honking at kids they're here to pick up, mush into an echo. Under my hand, the bristly grass fused into a solid wood trap door.

The door opened with a gentle tug. If it was on school property, it must be safe. At least, that's what I would say if I got in trouble. It would only take me a minute to see what was behind the door. No one would even notice. I clutched my backpack to my chest to fit through the narrow opening, and crawled down the ladder.

I could smell the dirt and moist air as my toes reached down for each rung, one by one, hands gripping the rusty metal ladder in the pitch-black dark. I must have gone down an entire floor. I worried this would go on forever but then my foot hit solid ground. I stepped into the light.

"Is it your first time here?" There was a boy wearing a plain white T-shirt and slim jeans. He was waiting by the ladder like he was expecting me. "You can put your backpack in a cubby. The ball pit is straight ahead, and the craft rooms are down the hall." The boy had light brown hair and an easy smile. He looked familiar, but I don't think he was in my class even though we were the same age. It was a good thing I didn't recognize him because I didn't want to see any of those people.

I nodded, not wanting to let on that I know nothing about this place. I wasn't invited, and only came here by accident. I put my backpack in cubby No. 3. Hopefully, its owner wouldn't mind.

I leaned in to look inside the ball pit. It was like the ones at McDonald's, but much bigger. There was one girl, wearing a white fuzzy sweater that matched her hair, and pink cotton candy eyes. She was hopping and burrowing through the balls, then threw a ball into the air and watching it land. Even when I looked at her she didn't say anything. The ball pit looked like a good place for a nap, but first I wanted to see what else was here.

In the craft room there was another girl my age. She had loose blonde curls and bright blue eyes, and wore a periwinkle blouse tucked into a skirt with buckled shoes—a contrast to my oversized tie-dyed T-shirt and tapered leggings with slouch socks.

She sat at a bulky taupe sewing machine. On the wall next to her there was a grid of art.

"Are those your paintings?" I stepped closer to admire the ornate gold-framed canvases, with splotches of colors I recognized from my crayon set, like goldenrod and burnt sienna. Each one was a pile of scrunched-up multicolored scarves.

"Yes. Right now I just do colors, but eventually, I will make a flower." She eyed her work like she was unsure if any of the colors deserved to be made into a flower shape.

They were really cool even without being flowers.

She stepped on the pedal and the machine groaned as she moved the fabric through. I wanted to keep talking but the machine was loud, so I waited. And then I tried to think of something else to ask her, but my mind was blank.

"Do you know how to sew?" The blonde girl asked, cutting through the silence but keeping her eyes focused on her work. She pulled a bag up onto the table, filled with thread in every possible color.

"Yes. My mom taught me. We made sundresses one summer," I said. At the fabric store, we spent hours choosing a print. Mine was white with tiny yellow flowers and Becca chose navy with red flowers.

My response must have caught her interest—she looked up at me and giggled.

"Do you sew, too?" I said. That was a dumb question, she obviously did. I was thrilled we had something in common.

"I learned in Home Ec class." She licked the tip of a brown thread and leaned her head sideways to get a better view of the tiny needle so she could thread it.

"I don't think my school has that class," I said.

"I took it when I was older," she said. Now, with the needle threaded, she leaned over the machine, pulling the top and bottom threads away from her to stitch another seam.

"Whoa … you've been older before?" I said.

She sat down in the red plastic chair. "Yes. I have been older, and I have been younger," she replied. "But here, I am always the same age." She shrugged.

She got up and pulled a bundle of fabric from the shelf, a warm amber and chestnut design that looked like fall leaves, and paused, as if trying to remember something. "Everyone here is the same age."

"Oh, yes. I think you are right," I said, remembering the boy at the entrance. "What are you making?"

"This is a tablecloth for Thanksgiving," she said.

I nodded. Sewing was cool, but there were also books. I stepped up to the floor-to-ceiling shelves. The books were jumbled: a fishing guidebook next to a mystery novel, some of them seemed old and others newer. I didn't see any *Babysitters Club* or *Nancy Drew* novels, but I picked out a green-spined book and began to read from the first page. It was much thicker than *Bunnicula* so it must be for bigger kids, or even adults. The back said it was about a girl who visits her grandparents and goes through the gate to their neighbors, and finds out she traveled back in time 250 years. I leaned against the wall on a beanbag chair and started the first chapter.

When there was a knock on the door, I realized I was on page 86 already. "Hey, you, uh, ladies want to go for a tractor ride?" It was the boy by the entrance who told me about the cubbies, standing in the doorway. I looked at the blonde girl but she just blushed and giggled.

"I'm okay," I hollered from my corner.

"You're … okay?" he asked with a hopeful smile.

I corrected myself. "Oh, I mean, no, thank you." Maybe I was supposed to speak properly like I do at my grandparents' house. This wasn't home, even though I felt really comfortable.

I folded the page and crawled over to the plastic bins next to the bookcase. There were piles of colored construction paper, different kinds of pencils, and watercolors. I plopped down on the thick carpet with a set of graphite pencils and a drawing pad and sketched a picture of a farm with lots of animals, cows, pigs, chickens, and horses. My dad used to work summers at his uncle's farm in Kansas and they had a bunch of animals, but at my house we only have a bunny named Snowball who doesn't do anything but sit in her cage and try to dig a tunnel out.

When I finished, I held the picture up in the air to admire it.

"When you're done, you can choose a frame and put it on the wall," the blonde girl said. It didn't take too long to find what I wanted. I chose a red frame with cream-colored matting.

Between drawing and reading the book, I had no idea what time it was. Becca must have been waiting by the tree for hours. I hoped I wasn't in trouble. "I think I should go back, so my sister doesn't worry about me," I told the blonde girl.

"Okay," she said. "Bye!"

I walked myself out, pulled my backpack from the cubby, and crawled up the ladder.

Turns out, I had nothing to worry about. The world above was still frozen, and it wasn't until I closed the hatch that the blurry landscape popped back into movement.

Becca was waiting by the tree, book in hand. We walked side by side down the hill. She didn't notice the difference. I wanted to say something, I really did, but I was sure that a place like the Underworld was supposed to be secret, so I didn't let on I had been anywhere.

Besides, Becca would never believe me. She only read boring stuff like *Pride and Prejudice* and not fun things like *The Hobbit*.

We walked in silence. I looked around at the kids who didn't have a secret world of their own and felt sorry for them. I always knew I didn't belong here. Finally, I had a place where people understood me.

Mom's van wasn't at the park. We sat in the grass. Becca worked on her math homework, and I pulled out *Bunnicula*. I still wanted to know if the bunny would make it. But more importantly, I wished I'd written down the name of the old green book from the underworld so I could find it at the school library.

When Mom's van pulled up, I didn't want to go. Now that I had been to the Underworld, other places weren't as good. I was tired of being a mechanical monkey. School, home, dinner, sleep, repeat. I decided to stay in the park and finish my *Bunnicula* book and then maybe go back to The Underworld and finish my other book.

"Mom says you have to come now," Becca said on her second trip down the grassy hill.

"I'm not coming," I said. Becca sighed loud enough so I would know she was mad at me and walked back to the car.

She came back. "Mom says you're grounded."

I was fully immersed in my book so I didn't hear her. Well, mostly. I ignored her.

"Mom says you're grounded for a month," she said on her fifth trip. I thought about what that would mean for me, but couldn't think of anything fun we had coming up. Being grounded just meant reading more books. Becca tried to pick up my backpack and carry it up the hill herself, but I grabbed it and pulled so hard she lost her grip.

"*Lindsay!*" she screamed.

To be honest, I felt a little flustered, because I didn't know the rules of the Underworld and whether I could go back so soon. If I was wrong, I would have to spend the night in the park, which wasn't as pleasant as the beanbag in the sewing room. But if I went home, I would be grounded. There was no way to win.

Becca returned. "Mom's going to take your twenty dollars away," she said.

I got up without speaking. We didn't get an allowance, so that was all the money I had from my last birthday.

In the car, Becca worked on her math problems and I sat in the way-back row so I could be alone. She spent hours on her homework every night. I didn't have as much yet. Mom's preaching radio program was on and the pastor with the southern accent droned, "Sheep, they're dumb! And that's why Gawd uses sheep in the Bible so much. We humans, we're simple-minded, dull-headed…"

Mom didn't say anything to me on the way home and I wondered if I was in extra big trouble. Sometimes when I was really bad, she wouldn't punish me until Dad got home, and he would punish me instead, which was much worse. When we pulled into the garage, I stared at the old John Deere tractor nameplate hanging on the wall by Dad's truck, and wished I could rewind time, go back to the park, and not be bad.

In my room with the door shut, I found the art supplies in my dresser. Mom got them for me a long time ago but I had never used them. Since I was so good at drawing in the Underworld, I decided to draw the faces of everyone in my family. I captured each of our distinguishing features— Mom's curly hair, Dad's side part, and even though Becca and I had the same blond-streaked hair, you could see our different personalities in our eyes.

Dad tapped on the door in a half-knock that pushed it open. He was still in his work clothes, a button-up shirt, and slacks.

"How are you?" he asked.

"I'm okay." I looked back down.

"You're okay," he said. "It's usually 'good,' but today, you are 'okay.'"

I kept my gaze down.

"Still one word, though," he said as if this was a funny joke.

Why did he have to tease me? I didn't know what kind of answer he wanted me to have.

"Did you learn anything at school?"

"No," I said.

When I wandered out for dinner, everyone acted normal. From my chair in the corner by the window, I squinted at the artwork hanging above the couch in the living room. It was a painting of my mom and her sister when they were kids. She was wearing a dress with a rounded collar and a little bow, just like the one worn by the blonde girl in the underworld. Mom's hair was blond when the painting was done, but now she dyed it reddish brown and curled it with a hot brush shaped like a tube.

The next day at school, I stared at the clock. I wanted to go back to the Underworld. I thought about drawing a circle on the playground during recess or in the back of the classroom after I finished my handwriting test early, but I didn't know if it would work in different places. So I waited until school was over, until I was walking over the grass to the tree. I tried not to cringe as I kneeled—how weird would I look if I were wrong!

Just like before, the hatch appeared. I pulled my backpack to my chest and slid down the ladder, closing the hatch behind me. The boy was sitting in a chair, playing a guitar.

"Hi!" I said. I hoped he would remember me.

"Hello!" he smiled. "I'm just working on some chords. Want to hear them?"

"Sure," I said.

He strummed a few times, nodding his head. "That's a G," he said.

Then, he moved his fingers, and strummed a few more times, making a different sound. "That's A minor!"

"That's cool," I said. I moved on.

The blonde girl was in the craft room again, but this time she was painting colors. She had her brows furrowed like a scientist mixing chemicals, then burst into giggling. Must not have come out like she expected.

I pulled my book off the shelf, quietly so I wouldn't distract her, and sat in a big armchair to read. After a while, I thought I should ask her more about this place.

"Are there other people here?" I asked. I wondered if

she had other friends here, too, or if it was just me.

"Yes, sometimes," she said. "I see other people here sometimes, and then I don't see them for a while." She didn't seem too concerned about this. "But I do know that when they are ready to come here, they find it on their own," she said.

"Do you come here from school?" I asked. I had looked for her on the playground during the lunch period.

"No, I come from my backyard."

"Oh," I said. That surprised me. Maybe she lived near the school and used a different entrance. I hadn't gone further down the hallway, but I bet this place is huge!

"Can we be friends in real life … up there?" I asked. Wow, what a dumb thing to say! We barely knew each other. But she wasn't like my friends at school, who always wanted to play tag at recess. I was so bored of them and I don't like running. With her, I felt happy, even when we didn't talk.

She looked up at me, her mouth turned down. "I don't think we can," she said.

I pulled a chunk of hair into my mouth and wrapped it around my bottom lip. She probably knew better because she had come here more often than me, but I still felt rejected.

"I am happy we can be friends here, though," she said. She stopped painting for a moment. "Do you want to watch a movie?"

"Okay," I said.

I followed her further down the dark hallway. The walls were made of mud and lined with powder blue doors on either side. We passed four doors before we got to the one she wanted. The hallway kept going further, so far that I couldn't see how many more doors there were. Inside the room there was a huge fireplace, twice the size of my closet, with a brick hearth and a heap of extra wood pieces. It crackled steadily like revolving sprinklers on the lawn. The TV had a VCR attached to it like the ones I've seen at rich people's houses.

We wrapped ourselves in a blanket by the fireplace and turned on *Lawrence of Arabia* because she said it had nice music.

The blanket was so soft and warm. This place really had everything. There were art supplies, a bookshelf, even musical instruments—and I hadn't checked out the other rooms or played in the ball pit yet!

"Do you like me?" the blonde girl asked.

"What? Yes, of course." I said. I wasn't saying it only to be polite. I felt so peaceful with her. Even though we only just met a day before. She was the best friend I've ever had.

The last thing I remember was a camel walking over a massive sand dune. When I woke up, everyone was gone and the underworld was dark. I made my way back up the ladder to the same old daylight and my other life. Walk with Becca to the park. Van ride home. Homework.

Except I couldn't be normal anymore, because the Underworld changed me. I stretched out on my bed. I wasn't in the mood for music, even though I had my own CD player and some CDs. I listened to the silence and laid perfectly still. There was a scrape in the popcorn ceiling. It was there as long as I could remember. I thought about my friends in school and whether there was an entrance to the Underworld on the football field at school so I could leave at recess when my friends played tag. Mom peeked her head in.

"Hi honey," she said. "What are you doing?"

"I'm thinking," I said.

"Is everything okay?" she asked.

"Yes," I said. A few hours had gone by and I hadn't started my homework yet. Maybe it wasn't normal to daydream for so long. I should at least make it look like I was doing something. I pulled my social studies book out of my backpack and opened it next to me so I could pretend I was reading if someone came in again.

Dad tapped on my door. "Dinner time!" he said.

"Okay!" I yelled. I jumped off the bed and walked to the kitchen. The plates were set out on placemats, with a saucepan of peas and carrots on a potholder, and a bigger container with beef stew, next to the ceramic bunny rabbit and wicker basket overflowing with green cellophane grass and foil-covered chocolate eggs.

"Did you wash your hands?" Mom asked.

"Yup," I said.

"Are you sure?"

"Yes." I rolled my eyes.

"Linds, you didn't have time to. Dad just told you it was dinnertime. Go do it now," she said.

I sighed as loud as I could and went to the bathroom, flipped on the light, and observed myself in the mirror. I waited. Then, I walked back to the kitchen.

"Did you wash them?" Mom said. "Let me smell." She took my hands and sniffed them. "You didn't wash your hands!" She looked at my dad in astonishment. "Go and do it for real!"

I walked down the hall to the bathroom and contemplated my options. There was the sink and the hand soap. There was also a decorative tin of body powder on the counter that someone had gotten for Christmas once. I opened it, tapped some of the powder onto my hands, and rubbed it around. Triumphant, I walked back to the kitchen and presented my hands to Mom.

"Is that baby powder?" She laughed. "You know I'm just going to make you go back and do it again." I looked at my dad for help.

"Honey, we're all waiting to eat," Dad said. "Our food's getting cold." He always took her side. It was some sort of code they had.

"Fine!" I walked back to the bathroom. I should have

known she could smell the powder. I was out of ideas on how to escape the routine of hand-washing, a failure. I came back and slid behind Becca's chair to get to my seat.

The phone rang. Becca leapt up to make a mad dash for it. Sometimes we raced.

"Let the answering machine get it," Mom said, cutting Becca off when she was inches from the phone.

"But what if it's *Grandma*!" Becca said.

"Then we can call her back. We're having dinner," Mom said, scraping more vegetables onto my plate than I wanted.

After everyone was done eating, I was assigned to rinse and load the dishwasher.

"Here, put an apron on so you don't splatter your school shirt." Mom handed me a red one from the hook inside the pantry door. The pattern was of different kinds of fruits. "I made that in my Home Ec class," she said.

"You had a Home Ec class?"

"Yeah, it was in high school. I guess they don't do that anymore, though!" She rustled my bangs before stepping into the family room to close the blinds.

I used the stainless steel scrubber to wipe the food remnants off each plate and considered this new development. How did my friend in the Underworld take a Home Ec class if they don't do it anymore? Maybe that's what she meant when she said she had been older and younger.

When I turned off the sink I could hear my dad playing

his bluegrass music and whistling on his harmonica. He had an attachment that bolstered it above the guitar. I wondered if the boy from the Underworld was learning more chords.

In my room, I shut my door and turned on a CD to drown out my dad's bluegrass playing. There was something I forgot in the kitchen. I walked back out, but just before I stepped onto the tile, I saw my mom standing by the sink, staring out the window into the backyard. It was dark outside so I didn't know what she was looking at. Not our rabbit— the bunny cage was on the other side of the backyard.

I couldn't ask mom if she knew about the Underworld. She would think I was crazy, and then I'd be one of those kids who gets taken out of class to see the school counselor and people would think there was something wrong with me.

I went back down the hall to my room. Oh, a glass of water, that's what I went to the kitchen for. But since Mom was there, I pulled my portrait drawings from the art drawer in the dresser. It was clear that I was very talented. Each of the faces felt so alive. I brought them back to the kitchen, and stepped across the carpet border onto the tile. Mom was still staring at the yard.

"Mom?" I said. "Look, I drew our family."

She examined each drawing. "Cute, honey. But why are our faces sagging?" She laughed.

I inspected the drawings again. Now that she mentioned it, I could see that all of our ears were along our jaws, lower on the face than they should be. We did look like we were sagging.

Back in my room, I put the drawings away and shoved the drawer shut. Maybe I wasn't very good at drawing. I wanted to go back to the Underworld. My drawing of the farm was better. I remembered all the animals looking so realistic.

My stuffed pigs sat in the antique baby crib facing me, and my backpack was on top of the bookshelf. A few shoes seeped out of the small closet, but otherwise, the floor was clear. I could draw a circle, right here on the carpet. But when I entered the Underworld before, I was on grass. Would it work?

Just because the blonde girl could go from her backyard didn't mean I could go from my bedroom.

There was no guarantee I could go again. Maybe it was only open on certain days. No one told me the rules. I couldn't bear the thought of trying to enter and failing. That would make the whole thing seem like it was just a fantasy. That would mean I was just a silly child, not very smart, and not deserving of a secret underworld where everything was perfect. I put on my pajamas and crawled under the covers.

At school tomorrow, when I cross the grass to the tree, I'll keep my eyes straight ahead and not even sneak a look for the lines in the grass. I needed to believe I had been there, even if it meant never going back.

The Archeologist

Shauna Alderson

"Making my rounds of the ruins
　　　　Ancient as the earth
　　　　Dust motes catching sunlight
Brown eyes catching glimpses
Of invisible forces
Forever at work
Overgrowth crunching underfoot
Vines creeping patterns
Suspended in time
They give a wide berth
To memories buried here
Sunken beneath soil
Treasures and trinkets
I call inner work
Sun pours into sweat

Shovel uncovers the cache

Stashed by the Child

Who was here first

Making the rounds of my ruins

A phoenix's rebirth   55

Pirate Piper

Anne J. Hill

When I was eleven years old, my sister, Arietta, and I spent a lot of time with Uncle Jazper. He'd sit us down in the drawing room and tell grand stories about our father and his friends. Uncle Jazper would pace about the room, waving his arms as he acted out what he spoke. He'd even make funny voices so each person sounded different. He and Arietta would spend days running around the woods and creating stories about fairies and wild people. I'd sit by a tree and watch, sometimes bringing a book.

"Piper!" Arietta ran over to me and tugged at my hand. "Come play!"

I yanked my hand back with a frown. "I don't want to."

She pouted. "You used to play with me."

"Someone has to make sure you and Uncle Jazper don't get hurt, tramping about the woods like deer."

Her lower lip quivered, and I knew I had gone too far. "Why are boys so mean?" she cried.

I let out a long sigh. "Arie, I'm sorry." I pushed myself up to stand and placed my hand on her shoulder.

She sniffled and wiped snot away from her nose. "I just want my brother back."

"I'm sorry." But I still didn't want to play. I slid back down into my seat against the tree.

She turned and ran off, shouting, "Uncle Jazz, Uncle Jazz! He said no!"

He gasped and looked at me and whispered something to Arietta. He trotted over, crouched to my eye level, and put his hands on his knees. "Hey, Piper. I really need your help. There are pirates about to attack our ship, and we need another strong man to ward them off."

I quirked my eyebrow. "Weren't you a pirate in real life? You can handle it."

Uncle Jazper slowly grinned. "Aye, I was, matey. A real fearsome, trick you like a baby, sword-wielding, money-thieving pirate!" His playful look faded slightly. "Your father was a pirate once, too, you know."

"Well, I'm Piper. I don't like pirates, or guns, or fighting, or pretending, or adventures, or any of that rot." I picked up the book by my side and cracked it open.

Uncle Jazper sat down in front of me. "What are you reading?"

I turned the cover towards him. "*Meno and the Wasteland.*"

He grinned at me again. He was always grinning. "You know, that is a pretty adventurous dragon book. You said you don't like adventures, but you're reading about them. Reading is a wonderful form of entertainment, but why not also live adventures? Or make your own up?"

I blinked at him. "Because adventures get people hurt."

"Who taught you that?"

"You did," I replied.

For once, Uncle Jazper looked off balance. "I did? How did I manage that?"

I shrugged. "All your stories. People always get hurt. And those are true stories, right? If everyone had just stayed home, no one would have gotten hurt."

His face wrinkled. "That was never the intention behind my stories. Yes, some people might have made poor choices and been reckless, but that doesn't mean all adventures are bad. Not all end in pain, especially not the pretend kind. You're not going to get hurt by helping me save this imaginary ship from fake pirates."

I sighed. "Half an hour, and then I'm reading my book again." I took his hand and let him pull me to my feet.

"Deal."

I carefully situated my book on the tree's roots and followed him over to Arietta.

"Piper! Look!" She held her hand out to show me a blue

jay chirping on her palm.

"That's great, Arie." She was always showing me animals. It's not that I didn't like animals, but there are only so many times someone can be impressed by the same thing.

She giggled when the little bird pecked at her dark brown braid. "He wants to make a nest out of my hair!"

"So where are these fake pirates?" I looked at Uncle Jazper.

"You have to get on our ship before you can see the pirates! This way." He scrambled over to four sticks that outlined a rectangle on the ground and stepped in.

Arietta ran after our uncle and stopped outside of the 'ship.' "Uncle Jazz! I need help getting in!" She held her arms up. He bent down and scooped up my eight-year-old sister and set her inside. They both looked at me. "Come on, Piper!" Arietta called.

I trudged over. "I don't need help getting in," I stated as I stepped over the stick, sliding my hands into my front pockets.

"Welcome aboard The Four Sticks, you scallywag!" Uncle Jazper placed a flimsy stick in my hand. I assumed it was meant to be my sword. I just nodded.

"Oh no! Look!" Arietta pointed up at the trees. "Pirates in the trees!"

"There aren't trees in the ocean," I pointed out.

Arietta turned to look at me. "Well, maybe there are in my pretend world."

"But that doesn't make any—"

Uncle Jazper interrupted, "We're not at sea currently. Our ship hit land on a faraway island, and there are pirates here, and they climbed the trees to see who we are."

"Wait, aren't we pirates too?" I remembered being called a 'scallywag' and frowned.

"Er, that we are, matey! But these are enemy pirates! They want to steal our boat and sail away!" Uncle Jazper scrambled to fix the flawed logic I had pointed out.

"Couldn't they just—"

"Piper, stop it!" Arietta shouted at me. "This is no fun." She crossed her arms, pouting.

I looked down, feeling bad. "Sorry, sorry. I'll stop talking."

Uncle Jazper sighed. "You can keep talking. Just try to use more of that imagination I know you have."

I nodded, but I wasn't as sure as him.

Uncle Jazper gasped and looked up at the sky. "Oh no! Look! Dragons! Flying everywhere!" He pointed at the clouds.

I looked up and squinted hard to see the fake dragons. One of the tree branches did sort of look like a dragon if I didn't think about it too much. It could even look like smoke was coming from its mouth because of the clouds behind it. I shuffled a little and then said, "I see a brown dragon."

Uncle Jazper put a hand on my shoulder. "Aye, I see it too, matey. What should we do about these fiery beasts?"

I fiddled with the stick in my hand, trying to pretend it

was a sword.

"I think we should befriend the dragons!" Arietta squealed.

Uncle Jazper squinted at the sky. "Do you reckon they're friendly dragons? I think perhaps they wish to burn our ship down. What say you, Pirate Piper?"

"Um." I thought a moment. "Arietta could try to befriend it first, but if it tries to hurt us, then we attack it?" I wasn't too certain that was the right answer.

"Brilliant plan, Pirate Piper! I like your courage. Pirate Arietta, what say you?"

Arietta grinned and nodded fast. "Operation Befriend Dragon underway!" She jumped out of our little ship and marched up to the tree-branch dragon. "Hello, great fire-breathing dragon! Would you like to be my friend?"

Uncle Jasper cupped his mouth and, in his best dragon voice, bellowed, "Hello, little girl! If you have chocolates, I will be your friend. If not, I'll burn your ship down!"

Arietta giggled and said, "Oh no! We don't have any chocolates." She turned and ran back to our ship. "He's going to get us!"

I watched the dragon closely and pictured all the pirates sitting up in the trees, swinging their swords. "Maybe we can befriend the enemy pirates, and they can help us defeat the monster?"

"There's a plan!" Uncle Jazper said with a pat on my

back. "On you go, Pirate Piper. Operation Befriending Pirates is your job."

I hesitated, then stepped out of the stick ship and looked at the trees. "Hello. Um. Pirates. Would you work together with us to defeat the dragon?" I felt a little silly talking to empty trees, but I tried to pretend there were pirates listening closely.

"If you have any ice cream, we will help you!" Uncle Jazper spoke as if he were the tree Pirates.

I frowned. "We don't." I ran back to the ship. "They won't help us without ice cream. Maybe we can use the dragon to scare them away?"

Uncle Jazper's eyes lit up. "Another excellent plan! If the dragon chases us, we can lead him right to the pirates, and they will run away screaming. And then we can focus on defeating the dragon."

"Waves your hands!" Arietta said as she flung her hands in the air. "Here, dragon dragon!"

I slowly lifted my hand. "Come here, dragon."

Uncle Jazper jumped up and down, waving both his hands fast. "Oh, dragon! Follow us!"

I smiled a little. He looked so silly doing that, but he didn't seem to care.

"Quick! Row the ship. The dragon is coming!" Arietta screamed and pretended to row. I copied her, and we sailed the boat toward the tree pirates.

The pirates screamed when they saw the dragon. They climbed down the trees and ran off into the forest, tripping over tree roots and leaves.

"Woohoo!" I shouted. "The other pirates are gone. Now just the dragon left." I gripped the sword in my hand and glanced over my shoulder at the brown dragon blowing a blast of fire toward us. "Turn the ship around!"

"Aye, aye, Pirate Piper!" Uncle Jazper saluted, turned the ship around, and aimed us directly at the dragon.

I stood at the ship's highest point and looked the dragon in the eyes. "Dragon! This is your last chance to be our friend! Attack us again, and we will fight you!" My heart raced. What if I got hurt? I shook my head and narrowed my eyes; determination flooded me. I had a sister and goofy uncle to keep safe, and no dragon, real or fake, was going to hurt them.

The dragon laughed. "You don't have any chocolate. And besides, I happen to like burning down pirate ships and gobbling pirates whole." He let out another blast of fire and swooped for us.

I swallowed. "You're not allowed to hurt my family!" I lifted my sword in the air, and as the dragon swooped down on us, my blade nicked his wing. He let out a loud roar in pain, fluttered, then tumbled into the water.

"Is he dead?" Arietta asked.

I leaned over the edge of the ship to look and shook

my head. "No. He's just hurt. Look. He's swimming away. I don't think we have to worry about him coming back again."

Uncle Jazper clasped my shoulder. "Not with Pirate Piper on board. All dragons should fear attacking the Four Stick Ship! But also, maybe we need to buy a bunch of chocolate and ice cream." He winked.

I chuckled and then frowned as the sword in my hand shifted back to a stick. I looked over my shoulder and watched the dragon fade into the dirt ground. Something warmed in my chest.

But then my hand stung. I noticed I had been holding onto my stick too hard, and it made my palm bleed a little.

"Uh oh." Uncle Jazper looked at my hand.

I shook my head. "I told you I would get hurt." I grinned at him. "But that's okay. It was worth it to fight a dragon and save my family." I puffed out my chest, feeling a surge of excitement I never fully got from just reading by a tree. This was my own story, even if it was just pretend. I'd been brave, and maybe if I could defeat imaginary dragons, I could also overcome the real scary things in life.

A Nathal Short Story

My Thoughts Linger Here

Willow Whitehead

The world in a fenced in backyard
Magic confined as a safeguard
A flower garden or a forest
Birds forever nearby chorused
The pebbled path leading here
Flowers grow new year by year
A shadow dashed through the pond
Rocks speak of creatures now long gone
The wooden bench stuck in its nook
Ferns surround what they overtook
A child sat upon the ground
She comes there when overwound
The scent of cookies on the wind
Beckons her to come back in

Playing Pretend

Hannah Carter

This smells, Ana!" Mabel squirmed away from her cousin's prodding fingers, but Ana held the girl firm with one hand embedded in Mabel's frizzy red locks. Ana dunked her hand into the murky water of Puck's Marsh and scrounged along the bottom to come up with another fistful of mud. "Well, goblins aren't exactly known for their hygiene, so if you want to be a proper one, shut up." Ana's words were slightly garbled by her grandmother's silver locket, which she held between her teeth. Mostly because her mouth kept the jewelry clean—but doing so also helped her to concentrate. And concentrate she must! Applying the muddy makeup for their goblin mask was important.

"But I'm not a goblin. I'm a fairy. And fairies don't like sticky stuff." Mabel shuddered. "How come when we play pretend, I always get messy?"

"Because there's no better way to play, obviously."

Despite Mabel's wiggling, Ana scrubbed the brown goop on her cousin's fair cheeks. At last—Mabel looked truly ghoulish, save the ever-shimmering wings behind her. But since they were real, Ana couldn't do anything about them, lest she pluck them off. And she'd *really* get in trouble for that.

"Perfect." Ana sat down cross-legged in the reeds. Her long black hair snagged under her bum, both of which were wet. "Now, my turn. Make me look absolutely frightening." After all, even if it was just pretend, she had to look terrifying to march into war against the Lord of the Highland Elves, just like in the play her parents had recently performed.

Not to mention, if the Dragon King showed up today, she needed to be extra frightening to keep everyone safe.

Ana sucked in a deep breath to keep from inhaling some grubby piece into her lungs. Mabel's work was far more artistic. She dotted little glops of mud, traced patterns, and, finally, took both hands and rubbed them down Ana's face.

The air grew stale inside Ana's lungs, and she gasped and coughed. *Ew*—Mabel was right. Their costumes did stink.

But she could scarcely complain since she'd just chastised Mabel—not to mention that an actress on the theatre stage wouldn't whine. "Well? Do I look fearsome, like the Goblin Queen?" Ana twisted her mouth up and bared her teeth.

Mabel let out a delicate peep. "Oh! Yes. You're terrifying." She shuddered. "No wonder everyone was scared of her."

"I think they were scared of her because she killed a thousand men in one day and ate their bone marrow for supper."

"Well, it didn't help that she was ugly."

Ana cackled and flopped forward so that the marsh's reeds hid her from any passer-bys. "Now. We must stage a surprise attack on the Lord of the Highland Elves. We'll crush him beneath our huge goblin feet and make the rest of the world tremble in fear until a hero can appear!"

She crawled forward on her stomach, scarcely caring that she was getting mud and water all over her white dress. Things like that just wouldn't bother the Goblin Queen, anyway. Especially not when she had bone marrow—whatever that was—to eat.

"Ana—" Mabel began, flat on the ground a few inches behind Ana.

"Goblin Queen," Ana hissed.

"Goblin Queen, I'm getting all dirty. And it's hot. And it's lunchtime and I'm hungry. How much longer?"

Ana rolled her eyes, so it was a good thing she had taken the lead ahead of her cousin. Mabel didn't take well to eye-rolling. It usually brought on tears. "We'll go until we have defeated the Lord of the Highland Elves. A goblin will never surrender just because they are uncomfortable! They have impenetrable hides, huge tusks, and an awful smell designed to strike fear into their prey! They don't worry about if things are dirty!"

Mabel grumbled something, and it sounded an awful lot like: "Well, *I* do."

Ana almost turned around to deliver a rousing speech that would spur Mabel into a fierce warrior, but a yell startled her—right before a stick hit her head.

"How dare ye come this way, ye filthy Goblin Queen!" The owner of the third voice—a girl in a brown dress and oversized boots—jumped down from a tree limb and splattered Ana and Mabel with even more gunk. Mabel squealed, but Ana responded with her best roar…though it may have started out as a shriek.

"Lyn! You got me all wet!" Mabel whined.

Ana took a deep breath and broke character to chastise her cousin. "That's not Lyn. It's the Lord of the Highland Elves, the sworn enemy of the Goblin Queen. And you are my faithful goblin soldier, which means that he is your enemy."

Mabel sighed. "Sorry. I forgot."

By the blue blazes of Zangoff, Ana loved Mabel, but sometimes it was very obvious that she was only nine years old. Not a mature ten—double digits!—like Ana and Lyn.

But still, Ana did love her cousin very, very much, even if her imagination muscle wasn't very strong.

Ana turned back to Lyn. "You dare use your puny

arrows against me?" She roared once more and stomped her feet. She'd taken her papa's boots to mimic the heavy thumps of ginormous goblin feet. "You will die, as well as all the other elves!"

Lyn puffed out her chest, her voice low as she spoke. She was the best at boy voices, which was why she usually got to play all the boy parts. "Never! I am the Lord of the Highland Elves, and you shall not pass." She drew another stick and threw it at Ana. This time, though, Ana held up her hand. The stick never made contact—her magic stopped it in mid-air.

Ana swirled her finger around and the stick followed suit, as if the imaginary arrowhead now pointed at her best friend. "Puny—"

Lyn sighed. "Goblin Queen—you don't have magic!"

Ana blinked. "What?"

"Goblins don't have magic," Lyn insisted.

Mabel gasped as if Ana had just committed a cardinal sin against playing pretend. "That's right!"

"But—but—" Heat flushed Ana's cheeks. "Maybe the Goblin Queen did! It was so long ago—maybe she was part witch, just like me and you, Lyn."

Lyn shook her head. "Nuh-uh." A grin split her face. "Which means the arrow would have hit you."

As Ana lowered her hands, her weapon dropped, and she sniffed. "Fine. We'll pretend like it hit me, but I still have an impenetrable goblin hide."

"That's fine, but I, the Lord of the Highland Elves, still know your weakness." Lyn unsheathed a larger stick. "A magic-infused sword!"

Ana squawked as Lyn swung at her. "This isn't in the script!" With a yelp, Ana ducked out of the way. "The Goblin Queen defeated the Lord of the Highland Elves. Mama and Papa do the play all the time!"

"We're making up our own ending!" Lyn hollered. "It's more fun this way!"

She tackled Ana to the ground. They both tumbled into the reeds, and Ana's head ducked under the water for a brief moment. She came back up, sputtering and coughing, but with enough imagination to fuel the Goblin Queen's revenge.

"Now I'm calling on all the swamp mermaids to help me!" Ana wiggled free of Lyn and held up her hands. "Mabel, you're a swamp mermaid now!"

"*Oooh.*" Mabel clasped her hands together. "I bet they're a lot prettier than a goblin. And I bet they don't eat bone minnows or whatever." She scrunched up her freckled nose. "Or, wait. Maybe they would eat minnows."

Ana hoisted up another stick just in time to stop another one of Lyn's swings. "They need to come eat this infernal Lord of the Highland Elves!"

Mabel giggled as she ran over to the other girls. Lyn swiped at Ana and then turned to lunge at Mabel. Her make-believe weapon made contact with the latter girl's stomach, and Mabel gasped.

"Ana!" Mabel reached one pitiful hand toward her cousin before she slumped down into the marsh.

"Get up, Mabel!" Ana hit the top of Lyn's stick with her own. "You've got an impenetrable hide, remember?"

Mabel peeked open one eye. "Oh, yeah."

"No, you don't!" Lyn shot back. "You turned your goblin into a mermaid. Swamp mermaids don't have impenetrable hides."

"Well—maybe she's a goblin-mermaid—" Ana began, but a different sort of roar echoed across the marshlands.

"Lyn!" a deep voice thundered.

Lyn froze. Her back straightened, and her dark eyes slithered between Ana and Mabel.

Heavy thumps—so like a goblin footstep, but also unlike—pounded through the mud. A disgusting squelch followed each one, and Mabel reached out and grabbed Ana's hand.

"The Dragon King," Mabel squeaked.

"New game." Ana latched onto Lyn's arm and tugged her near. "The Goblin Queen and the Lord of the Highland Elves have called a truce because the Dragon King attacked."

"Lyn!" the Dragon King bellowed.

Ana yanked both her friends down with a giant splash.

Mabel whimpered.

"Move!" Ana whispered. "Stay together. My lord, though you have been my enemy, I swear that I will offer you the protection of my impenetrable hide and my swamp mermaid servant to aid in our escape. We will not let the Dragon King assassinate you and ravage your lands."

"Thank—I mean, aye." Lyn's fake accent faltered but came back in full force. "The elves of the Highlands will not forget this. Ye will always find sanctuary in the Highlands, and my bow will ever fly in your favor."

They crawled through the tall reeds as they pretended. Pretending made everything less scary, even running away. Well, kind of. A bead of sweat trickled down Ana's neck, but she wasn't *scared*. No, that was probably because the sun was so blazing hot in the afternoon sky.

"Please hurry," Lyn whispered.

"I'm trying," Ana hissed back. Her hands sank down into the mud with every movement, and the water tangled up her skirts.

The ground rattled as the Dragon King marched closer, but Ana couldn't see him. Which was good—if she couldn't see him over the reeds, then hopefully, he couldn't see them.

"You better come here!" His words flew over the girls like fire, and they almost carried the same amount of scorch. Ana urged her troops forward—until she thought of an idea.

"Mabel—we're going to pretend you're just regular old you for a second. A fairy, not a swap mermaid," Ana said. "I need you to shrink down and fly to safety."

"But—" Mabel started.

"No buts. Trust me. It's all just pretend." Ana stared at her cousin's pale face. Even Mabel's freckles seemed to disappear, and her eyes seemed wide.

Ana licked her lips and grimaced as she tasted the muck and marsh water. "I need you to fly back to the Goblin Kingdom and stay there. The Highland Lord and I will join you as soon as we have escaped the Dragon King's clutches."

"But what about—" Mabel said again.

"Shh." Ana shook her head. "This is the game, Mabel. I need you to go."

Mabel fidgeted. The steady stomps grew closer, and Ana gave her a final shove. Mabel sniffled, but even as she did so, her body grew smaller and smaller until she was only a tiny ball of light, no bigger than Ana's palm. Then Mabel's little ball floated away, far out of the reach of the Dragon King's massive jaw.

"Good thinking," Lyn whispered in her regular voice.

"Dragons are the sworn enemies of swamp mermaids. I had to do something quickly." Ana sat up straighter and held out her hands toward her best friend. "Hurry. Link hands with me."

"Lyn!" the Dragon King called. "When I get my hands on you…"

Lyn grasped Ana's hands, their palms forced together.

"What are we doing?"

"Think invisible thoughts," Ana said. "We're both part witch, right? We just have to think invisible enough."

"All right." Lyn swallowed. "We're invisible. We're invisible..." She muttered this under her breath. Ana tightened her grip and repeated it, though she preferred to do so mentally.

Invisible. We're invisible. The Dragon King will never find us.

Green and purple sparks flickered to life on their hands—green for Ana's magic and purple for Lyn's—until everything, hands and sparkles—began to disappear.

Invisible. Invisible. We're invisible. The Dragon King can't yell at stuff he can't see.

Lyn's visage flickered and then blinked out of view as the magic crept up and swallowed everything. Though Ana couldn't see herself fully, the parts she could see also had gone transparent.

Invisible. We're invisible. Just go away, Dragon King. Don't burn us. Don't see us.

Ana held her breath; she couldn't hear Lyn breathing, either. The Dragon King passed closer, closer...

"Lyn!" he growled. "You better not be playing with those fairy girls again!"

Lyn's invisible—but still tangible—grip tightened on Ana's hands.

Water splashed up against them as the Dragon King

lumbered by, mumbling to himself all the while. Ana squeezed her eyes shut.

Invisible. We're invisible. Go away. Go away.

The Dragon King's rampage drifted further and further away until Ana finally sucked in a long overdue breath. Beside her, she could hear Lyn do the same.

The faintest hint of Lyn's dark, curly braids began to reappear, flecked with sparks of the emerald and violet magic.

"Come on," Ana whispered. Multicolored glitter dotted her own skin as she stood. "We need to get you home before the Dragon King comes back to his cave."

◌

Soaked, grimy, tired, and scared, the girls finally made their way to the other side of the bog—to the imaginary Highlands—and to a tiny, two-story cabin. Ana shinnied up a large evergreen tree first, Lyn right on her heels, and pushed open the circular window, just big enough for the two of them to sneak in and out as often as they needed to.

Ana crawled in first and landed with an *oomph* on Lyn's bed. She rolled out of the way—though she left a trail of muck behind—so Lyn could jump next.

"Thanks for coming back with me," Lyn panted. She held one hand around her side as her shoulders heaved. "You didn't have to do that."

Ana swiped her hand underneath her nose and sniffed.

"Of course I did. We're best friends. That's what best friends do."

A smile flickered onto Lyn's face. "I'm so glad to have a best friend like you." She sat down cross-legged on her bed. "I'm sorry about Mabel."

"You don't have to be sorry. It's not your fault that your dad is always angry. Or that he hates fairies."

"I know." Lyn pursed her lips. "But dragons like to avenge their mates." She twiddled her thumbs, her eyes downcast. "And they don't like anyone they consider dangerous near their gold."

Ana's eyes drifted around the abandoned attic room. This certainly didn't look like a place a dragon would keep treasured gold. It looked more like a place a dragon would keep a prisoner: beside Lyn's bed, there was only a worktable which sat in the corner, a mirror and a vanity covered up by sheets, and a handful of trunks locked tight with forgotten valuables.

Silence fell between the two girls. Thoughts of goblins and elves danced around Ana's head—but mostly ones of dragons and swamp mermaids.

Or, in this case, spellcasters and fairies.

And, being part of each, Ana felt the strife in the depths of her soul.

"I know he only wants to keep me safe," Lyn started. She sniffed. "After Mama…" She faltered. "What if he finds out how much I play with you and Mabel and decides I'm not safe? He tells me all the time that no one can know we're here, or the fairies might come kill me, too…"

"Neither of us would say a word." Ana shook her head. "And even if we did, the Great War is over."

Lyn snorted—a sentiment Ana understood. The Great War might have been over between the fairies and spellcasters, but wizards and witches were only just tolerated in Jenkirre. Ana's own mother had been disowned and stripped of the fairy throne for falling in love with a poor wizard.

And Lyn's mother had been killed for that exact same reason.

None of it was right or fair, but Ana didn't want to just hate everyone that was a fairy like Lyn's father did now. She especially didn't want to hate Mabel—sweet Mabel, who would cry if she stepped on a flower.

"I'm worried he'll make us move soon. I know Papa doesn't want to be here anymore, but we don't have anywhere else to go." Lyn rested her chin on her fists. "And I don't want to leave you."

"You won't," Ana said fiercely. "We'll run away before that happens. We'll start a new game. We'll be—we'll be pirates. All on our own, together, on the run from the most dreaded pirate in all the seven constellations." She paused, only to add dramatically, "Captain Draconius Rex."

Lyn's eyes sparked with interest. "I'd be a star tamer, then. Aelita Starbright—no! Starfury."

Ana thought for only a second. "And I'm Eliza Swiftly. Fastest pirate in all the seven constellations. My cutlass will slice through any enemy before they have the chance to call for help."

Lyn grinned. "And I'm made of real stars and can use my magic to control them. I can even make them explode—like bombs!"

"Captain Draconius Rex will never be able to find us," Ana said. "You can come live with me forever. And we can grow up to be stage actresses, and Mabel can visit whenever she wants to, and…" Ana's voice sped up as her excitement increased. "…and everything will be perfect. We'll never, ever have to be separated and we can be together forever. Just you and me."

"Just you and me," Lyn repeated. "I like that."

She linked her pinkie around Ana's, and they curled them around like loops. Their own version of a pinky swear—like a circle, it had no end.

"I like this end to the story of the Lord of the Highland Elves and the Goblin Queen much better than the actual play." Lyn swung their hand back and forth. "One where they come together and become best friends forever. And I bet peace came to the land because everyone learned to work together and not kill each other."

"I don't know. I still like it when the Goblin Queen devours the Lord of the Highland Elves' bone marrow in the play." Ana tilted her head, and her black hair spilled over her green eyes. "But this ending isn't bad, either."

"Do you think…maybe one day…the dragon will learn to be friends, too?" Lyn's lip twitched downward. "And stop hating the swamp mermaids and blowing fire at everyone?"

"I think so." Ana turned to look out the window. The sunset poured through the glass pane and bathed the two girls in hues of yellow, pink, and purple. "But if he doesn't, we'll just take the ship and disappear into the stars forever."

"Lyn!" The Dragon King's voice rattled the house. "Are you in here?"

"Go!" Lyn shoved Ana toward the window. "I'll be fine. He'll only yell at me a little." She slipped over and pushed several trunks onto the trap door, the one way the girls had to make sure the Dragon King wouldn't get in.

"Are you sure?" Ana whispered.

"Yes." Lyn shooed Ana. "It's okay. Promise. I'm Aelita Starfury. I can handle Captain Draconius Rex, but if he sees Eliza Swiftly, she'll be thrown in the brig for sure."

Ana put one foot on the windowsill. "Don't worry. Eliza Swiftly isn't afraid of the brig, but she can't risk being held prisoner right now. She has to go ready the boat and make sure the swamp mermaids are safely aboard." She paused. "I'll see you later. Come as soon as you can, okay?"

Lyn nodded. "I will. Go—I have to get changed before he sees me like this." She gestured to her ruined clothes.

"Okay." Ana dangled on the windowsill, one leg in and one leg out. "I love you, Aelita Starfury. My Lord of the Highland Elves."

Lyn dipped into a deep curtsey. "And I love you, Eliza Swiftly. My fair Goblin Queen."

With one more wave, Ana leapt back onto the tree and closed the window behind her.

Lyn was home and safe, back in the Dragon King's lair for the time being. But she wouldn't stay there. She was far too clever for that.

And there were plenty of adventures left, with forever to pursue them, together.

Imaginary Friends

Rachel Lawrence

Some kids had one
But I had three
Companions
Brought to life by me
We took adventures
In my mind
The four of us
Could always find
Something to do
On rainy days
I wrote the scripts
A thousand ways
And I would never
Feel alone
With comrades
Of my very own

Invention

Is the child of play

Not necessity as

Some may say

At what age

Do we lose our wonder

And find our whimsy

Buried under

Weighty responsibility

The harsh check of

Reality?

That trio taught me

Way back then

What I have had

To learn again:

Hold tight to the gift of

Creation

And befriend your

Imagination

Howl's Duet

K. DeCristofaro

I am someone
      who has never been afraid
      and it begs the question:
Am I brave?
or is there simply nothing to fear where
I've kept myself alone in the hat shop?

Alone in the hat shop
one begins to feel emptiness settling
inside the brim
one begins to feel ugly, even
and worn
and the hats are always new and must be
beautiful

day in day out day up and day under

Until I found myself with him
and learn
change does not scare me
for look what change has brought
and time does not scare me
for suddenly I have none to lose
and darkness does not scare me
for the darkness inside and all around
him is somehow more beautiful than
the daylight I bathe in
nothing to fear indeed
and more full of dreams than
a hat could ever be

You see? I ask

I show him the hat and
I show him the bucket and
I show him the time and
I show him myself and
if that is not enough then

day in day out day up and day under

I will show him again.

I am the one
     who reached out to
     grasp the starlight that bounced
off her reflection, and that
spark in the dark I wasn't so sure I saw
became the sole hope I could hold
in my palm against my heart.

She will be the last light of winter
She will come through the
crack in the doorway
She will catch on the back of my shirt collar

but the years move through me
and the days press on me
my conviction is missing
and my lost battles haunt me

The sun is setting
The door is closing
And I am falling
fast

Where is she?
I fear I may stop asking soon.

but under each stone
and through every window
and around the next corner
I am looking for you everywhere.

And so, I act

She shows me her body
and she shows me her mind and
I show her the turning
of this great big world

And though the years move through me
and the days press on me

she stays, to show me again.

Butterfly Playtime

Cristina Benavides

A cherished moment of you with us lived through a tiny lens that now resides in the haze of my memory. I believe it was on a partially cloudy day, though the weather could've been different. If it was clear outside, the light of the sun must've never stung our eyes. If it was cloudy; the coating in the sky must've been a light layer that hid us from the piercing sun.

Mom took my older sister and me to your yellow-brick school, just across the street from your two-storied white-with-red-trimmings house. We picked you up, you probably dropped off your school stuff, but you didn't change out of your white uniform polo shirt and navy blue pants. Then we walked down three blocks towards a small city park as if the four of us were the only ones out in the world. No cars rushed by, no dogs accompanied their owners, and no other kids rushed out of school into their homes, or to the park's building for after-school programs. It was just us between the towering statues that people lived in, the quiet still road felt like everyone in the world slumbered as we had our fun down at the park.

The city grounds were only a block long, with a tan-brick building and a public pool that separated the grassy field from the playground area. We made our way along the black steel-bar fence that wrapped around the park, passed the field where dogs fetched sticks, and straight to the playground. Back then, the playground area stood on raised earth coated in jagged wood chips and cool dirt, with metal-made jungle gyms and hollow molded plastic props. Grass and trees surrounded the potted island, with curved walkways that flowed through the greenery like conjoining rivers.

I don't remember what we did to entertain ourselves until we noticed the monarch butterflies. They weren't always there, they caught us by surprise as we played. Five or ten of them fluttered around us, as if they wanted to join in on our fun. We trailed them with our eyes and kept a lookout for their wide orange and black splayed wings. We'd invite them over by reaching out our arms, their weightless bodies balanced on our hands as their tiny legs tickled our skin. My sister hesitated and twitched at the butterfly's touch. While we quietly embraced, she swallowed her fears to join in on the fun.

Although we each held at least one, they all seemed entranced by you the most. Maybe it was your bright white polo shirt, it might have shined like a lighthouse in a storm to the monarchs on that cloudy day. Maybe you had some sweet fruit for lunch and the natural sugar still coated your fingers. They landed on you like you were a flower to rest on, with total trust and soft bliss. The monarchs must have felt that same alluring homely energy you naturally radiated.

The video in my memory plays the moment when you rested on your knees like a monk, with outstretched arms as if you were embracing the sky, as you craned your head upwards with beaming eyes and a calm, wide, grin on your face. You shifted your neck and hips to find the butterflies as they briefly landed on you on and off. You allowed yourself to be their playground as they bounced from your fingers to your arm, to your shirt, and to your head. My mom, sister, and I watched diligently with held breaths, waiting to see where they'd land. We let out a cheer at one point when one landed on your left palm. It stretched out its grand wings slowly, as though it were giving them a good stretch after a workout.

The butterflies eventually drifted away in the winds and carried on with their own adventure. One by one, they each landed for the last time and batted their wings 'goodbye'. The last butterfly flew off of you and I tried to trace it with my camera lens. My manufactured eyes caught nothing, but my natural eyes spotted its path just out of sight as I said 'ah, there it went,' I then turned to my sister, maybe to tell a joke, or to show her where the butterfly went. But the moment I uttered her name, she screamed in childish terror, the footage caught her feet as she scurried away, and we laughed in surprise. I accidentally scared her into thinking that the butterfly was going toward her when she least expected it.

The memory got caught in my old cherry chocolate cell phone, where it lay dormant in the slumbering casket of circuits and buttons to this day. Yet I watched it so many times that I remember the moment exactly like the camera footage. Do you have memories like that? Do you see it as the clips we made, but remember behind the scenes too? Do you remember the monarch butterflies?

Nightlight Quests

Anayis Der Hakopian

When we were younger, we did not have a garden

Or trees with strong branches to climb up as daunting towers

Instead, our adventures took place in nighttime-crafted forts

Made up of every scavenged pillow and blanket roll

To build our own little world under torchlight's warmth

Making up tales inspired from the lines of open book pages

With wobbly swords and handmade feathered masked faces

Fighting off demons that chased at the edges of the dark

Laughing and giggling over heros' fights and villains' losses

Left shocked, stuck in suspense over their twists and

tumbled ends

All whilst questioning where the monsters really did their hiding

Under beds and sticky floorboards or stalking inside the walls

Groaning in the dead of night to scare us senseless

To make us braver in our dreams and shield us from the creaking

Underneath the green glow speckles of ceiling stars

We braved our own set scattered journeys

Packed with our swords, masks, and spellcasting

To sneak our way through the dead of the house

Playing out quests as skilled thieves and dragon rescuers

With the company of happy four-legged wagging friends

Returning to our blanket forts with treasure troves

Of kind beasts, gleaming jewels, and lost abyss things too

And sustenance of snacks that should have stayed abandoned

Wondering if we can capture that magic and make it everlasting

Even grown those moments hold a taste of enchantment

We grew in nightlight quests and blanket fort building

Chasing off fearful shadows with a flicker of daring

And a promise that this small slice of a vast turning world

Will always just be ours for the taking in our creative dreaming.

Authors

Kathryn Reilly

By day, Kathryn helps students investigate words' power; by night, she resurrects goddesses and ghosts, spinning new speculative tales. Enjoy poetry in Shadow Atlas, A Flight of Dragons, Last Girls Club, Willow Tree Swing, Paris Morning and fiction in Tree and Stone, Seaside Gothic, Diet Milk, Blink Ink, and Apologue of the Immortals. Her rescue mutts, Savvie and Roxy Razzamatazz, hear all the stories first. When she's not writing, she's rewilding her suburban backyard. Twitter: @Katecanwrite

Alison Clarke

Alison Clarke is a poet and fantasy author who is also the Amazon #1 bestselling author of *Phillis: A Poetry Collection*, and the award winning young adult fantasy trilogy, *The Sisterhood*. Alison believes that stories can change the world.

Xanna Renae

Xanna Renae loves daydreaming about how to save her characters from the messes she puts them in. Currently she is giving life to the ideas inside her head from rural Missouri where she lives with her husband, Noah, and cat, Maestro. She has a bachelor of arts in Creative Writing from Southern New Hampshire University, where she graduated with highest honors.

When she isn't writing you can find her tucked away in her little bungalow reading, snuggling with her cat, or playing video games with her husband.

Find her online talking about writing, publishing, and life with chronic illnesses just about everywhere @XannasBooks or on her website XannaRenae.com

B.R.R *Cannon*

B.R.R. Cannon has always loved writing and storytelling. While fantasy and sci-fi are her staples, she also dabbles in other genres including poetry and nonfiction. She has previously published flash fiction with Spark Flash Fiction and Havok, and she's currently working on her debut novel and an inspirational nonfiction work. When she's not creating imaginary worlds, she enjoys drinking Darjeeling, finding excuses to wear costumes, and spending time with her husband, children, and cat.

Natasha Alva

Natasha Alva is currently a chemical engineering student who enjoys writing poems. Poetry became an unexpected hobby for her as she discovered it during the pandemic as a way to relieve stress from schoolwork and express bottled feelings. Through poetry, she gets to write stories and hopefully inspire people to appreciate literature in the form of writing. You can connect with Natasha on Instagram at @theburiedpages where she posts her poems. Some of her poems are currently featured in the Balm 2: Poetry for Beautifully Broken Souls and Magkasintahan 2.0 Volume VII.

Dani Fankhauser

Dani Fankhauser is a writer and meditation teacher, with work in Refinery29, Well+Good, The Cut, PopSugar, The Billfold, and Mashable. Her fiction has been published by HAD, Sheepshead Review, and Nightshade Publishing. She received an M.S. in journalism at Medill School of Journalism and B.A. in business at Point Loma Nazarene University. She resides in southern California with her senior rescue chihuahua, Bambi, and is working on a speculative novel.

Shauna Alderson

Shauna Alderson is a multimedia creator and energy healer. She is the author of Paragon (young adult fantasy) and A Heroine, Complete (poetry). Whimsical wordsmith, mystical musician, and nocturnal navel-gazer, she also studied International Development at the University of Calgary before plunging into the arts. When not creating, Shauna can usually be found growing too many indoor plants, devouring too much chocolate, and jamming to just enough K-pop. She currently lives in Alberta, Canada, with her family and rampant imagination. Check out her website at shaunaalderson.com.

Anne J. Hill

Anne J. Hill is an author who enjoys writing fantasy for all ages. Her love of words has led to her career as an editor and content writer. She runs Twenty Hills Publishing with the help of her circus performing best friend, Lara E. Madden. She spends her days dreaming up fantastical realms, researching ways to get away with murder…for writing, arguing over commas at the kitchen table, talking out loud to the characters in her head, promising her housemate that she isn't, in fact, crazy, and rearranging her personal library—affectionately dubbed the "Book Dungeon."

Willow Whitehead

Willow Whitehead has a love/hate relationship with writing, the words spill onto the page faster than she can type, or she'll stare at a blank document for hours. Though the words always come a bit easier in the middle of the night. Currently, she spends her days reading, drinking tea, and chasing her black cat, Z, through the woods.

You can follow her on Instagram as @WeepingWillowReviews and watch as she struggles to balance her time between work, rest, and her innumerable hobbies. Her previous publications include *The Willow Tree Swing* by Nightshade Publishing.

Hannah Carter

Hannah Carter is just a girl who loves to dream and write and still wakes up every day hoping to figure out she's secretly a mermaid. Her debut YA fantasy novel, Depths of Atlantis—filled with murder, magic, and, of course, mermaids—is out now through SnowRidge Press. Her short stories and award-winning flash fiction pieces have been published in over twenty anthologies. In 2022, her flash fiction piece, "A Home for Nova," won Havok's "Prismatic" anthology's Editors' Choice Award as well as a Realm Award. In addition to fiction, she also has had over a dozen devotionals published. In her spare time, she's probably either cuddling her cats, drinking tea, reading, or practicing for her imaginary Broadway debut. Connect with her on Instagram at @mermaidhannahwrites.

Rachel Lawrence

Rachel Lawrence writes from South Carolina, where she lives with her husband, four children, and no pets (despite the kids' constant campaign for one). She processes the world spinning around her and the thoughts swirling within her through stories and poetry. Her favorite poets range from King David to Elizabeth Barrett Browning to Taylor Swift. Her favorite Story is still being written.

K. DeCristofaro

K. DeCristofaro (she/her/hers) is a poet and multidisciplinary artist living in Boston, Massachusetts with her cat, dog, and partner. Frequent sources of inspiration include her Italian-American family, her long walks through New England wilderness, and her beloved adventures in roleplaying games. She is a hobbyist green witch, an herbal tea devotee, a horror film enthusiast, and a joyfully bisexual force of nature.

Cristina Benavides

Cristina Benavides recently graduated from Columbia College Chicago, majoring in Creative Writing. She also draws and often utilizes the two skills to make zines and a webcomic series. She spends her free time napping with her dogs, Waffles and Copper.

Anayis Der Hakopian

Anayis N. Der Hakopian is a British Armenian Director, Mix Media Animator and Writer based in London (UK). When she isn't stuck behind a computer screen she spends her free time writing poetry in the park whilst being mobbed by dogs.

Final Thanks

We would like to thank all of our authors for their wonderful submissions to this anthology. Without them, there would be no stories for us to share with you all.

We hope you've enjoyed this anthology, and that you look forward to future tales that Nightshade Publishing brings.

Thank You.